Moonst...
Pilgrim

Abhijit Palchoudhuri

NewDelhi • London

BLUEROSE PUBLISHERS
India | U.K.

Copyright © Abhijit Palchoudhuri 2024

For permissions requests or inquiries regarding this publication, please contact:

BLUEROSE PUBLISHERS
www.BlueRoseONE.com
info@bluerosepublishers.com
+91 8882 898 898
+4407342408967

ISBN: 978-93-5989-449-2

First Edition: January 2024

Moonstruck Pilgrim

Abhijit Palchoudhuri

Translated from Bengali by
Ananya Chatterjee

To

Anand Paul & Subrato Sarkar,

The duo who are more than my son

and

loving husbands of my two daughters.

Author's Note

Like any one in literary genre, an author often thinks of crossing the barrier of his own language to reach the readers of different languages of the world. In this age of globalization, it is felt more so as we are now living in a global village but speaking in different languages and unable to share creative thought, passions and feelings of one heart to another merely because of the inherent barriers of different languages. And, Thank God, we have at least one international language, English, which has made it possible to cross this hurdle.

Thus it triggers in me too a thought of translating my humble works of Bengali poetry and share my poetic emotions and passions with the international readers. And Ananya, the emphatic poet-soul I ever know, took up the cudgel and translated my fifty poems (selected from 3 of my published collections titled : *Nihsshim Udyaner Orchestra, Unplugged Mrityur Jharnatolay,* and, *Jyotsna Raate Sobai boney choley geley*) to my wonder so perfectly and beautifully that I became more fond of the translated versions than my original ones. Indeed, she did a marvellous job and I am indebted to her immensely for the same.

Rest with my dear readers to confirm and appreciate.

God bless.

Abhijit Palchoudhuri.

Translator's note

Language is only a medium albeit a powerful one. And when it comes to poetry, every language has its own unique nuance that it lends to the imagination and expressions of the poet as he or she is in the process of versifying the thoughts. The challenges of translating poetry are therefore quite different from the the challenges of translating any other form of literature. Before translating the poems of Abhijit Palchoudhuri, I had to first live his poems inside me. In Bangla we have a beautiful term for this – "Kobita Japon". I had to surrender myself and float in the imaginary world of every single poem before I could begin to render them in English. In that essence, this book has been a journey for me, a pilgrimage of sorts where, through his deeply reflective works I have discovered echoes of my own soul. I hope I have done justice to his art and have been able to maintain the same degree of pathos, mixed with zest in the translated poems. Abhijit Palchoudhuri's poems are honest, sincere, and straight from the heart. In my translations, I have tried to retain these inherent qualities. I am immensely grateful to the author for his confidence in my abilities as a poet and a translator.

For any lover of poetry, this collection promises to be a voyage worth embarking upon.

-**Ananya**

About the Book

The poems that appear in Moonstruck Pilgrim, have been chosen from three different Bengali poetry collections of Abhijit Palchoudhuri. The collection is not a random amalgamation of the individual verses. Rather, there is a subtle, loosely bound sequence which gently nudges the reader to begin a journey through the world of the poet and, in the process, discover their own universe and identity. The poems are housed in four different sections.

Section 1 - The Pilgrim

The Poet As The Seeker- The poems here are self-reflective, but they have a sense of restlessness, where the poet is the seeker and is impatient to find a meaning, a sense in the universe. There is hope, despair, and again hope in these verses as the pilgrim begins the inward journey

Section 2- Moon Drenched

The Poet As The Lover- The poems here, highlight Nature's role in shaping the soul and the sensitivities of the seeker. They are subtle, and soothing - and offer shelter to the weary pilgrim from the previous section.

Section 3- The Journey

The Poet As The Sailor - As the name suggests, this section depicts the journey itself- the experience gathered, and the priceless insight . The stormy obstacles, and the springs of light. Hope dying. Hope reborn. The voyage of the thirsty Self.

Section 4 - The Poet

The Poet As The Poet - In this section, the pilgrim, through the journey, has finally discovered the poet in him. The poet he always was. His identity. He's finally free.

It is not necessary to read the poems in sequence. The readers may choose to begin their journey from a different point altogether. And thus define their own pilgrimage.

Ananya Chatterjee

A dreamer is one who can only find his way by moonlight, and his punishment is that he sees the dawn before the rest of the world.

Oscar Wilde

Contents

The Pilgrim

The Man

(লোকটা)

He devoured all that was his.
Such was his lifelong hunger.

Ate his childhood, his toddler years.
His youth, the hours of marital bliss.
He ate away his household ties.
His entire life, eventually.

Such was his gluttonous appetite.
He devoured it all. All of it.
Religion
Education
Culture
Poverty.
He sunk his teeth and
ate into the very roots of democracy.
The continent, too, eventually.

Such was his endless appetite.
He kept devouring, even then.
Soil.
Water.
Wind.
Wilderness.
Villages too.

The entire civilization.
Eventually.

And yet
his ravenous cravings have stayed.
Waiting now to devour his Death.

Me v/s Me

(আমার সাথে আমার)

It's been a while since I met with me.
This man keeps raising a wall inside my body, all day long.

It's been a while
since I've had a word with me.
This man hasn't sung a song since long using the voice in me.

It's been that long since we have fought.
Since thc day
he began to sway his mighty iron rod. Yes, the man in me.

And now that the hour is close for me to part with me.
The man in me flies into the skies. I'm left - Solitary.

My Father's Paramour

(বাবার প্রেমিকা)

Baba had a lover from his college-days. She was a marvelous
singer.
Whenever the radio played her songs- Baba would listen –
transfixed,
in his armchair.
Rocking. Swaying. Gently.
Ma would bring
his morning tea.
Wiping off, her beads of sweat.
Hearing the song, she would gently smile-
The unadulterated smile of domesticity.
We'd watch them hum along, Tuning in with the radio song.

"Momo Chitte Niti Nritye Ke Je Nache"
The song of a dancing soul- Dancing until eternity.

We would watch them. We would listen. And we would grow up
little by little.

They would teach us how to split an egg in two
and mix it with rice for our meals. How to blow away
sorrow like dust flakes. How to distribute happiness like cakes.

Baba has since, left this world. Ma, in her withering eighties.
Even today, when that song is played somewhere, do I spot a
wetness glistening
in the wrinkled corner of her eye?

And I follow the firefly
in my hunt for that luminance. I race through the night-
like bygone days of innocence.

A game to end another game

(খেলা ভাঙার খেলা)

Every time I want to think of you- I end up thinking of rivers
instead-and paint an upstream flow
every time I begin your portrait.

In order to forget the agony you left-
Dolls of salt, I build and release into the ocean, I watch them
float to forget my trivialities-

I want to chisel an idol of you. But I break my idol in turn
One game always destroys the other-This it seems, I am yet to
learn!

The Adversary

(প্রতিদ্বন্দ্বী)

There was a tree I called mine. Born, perhaps,
in the same hours as I.

A tree that grew through infancy-
through the years of childhood just like me.

Years went by.
Youth came and I was told-You are no poet.
Become an engineer, instead!

And I complied. Got my degree. The tree merely stayed a tree.

And then,
when the saddest day arrived, I went to the tree,
wept all night.

In the waking hours of dawn I raised my head only to find a giant installation
of familiar wood scraping the skies.
Far, far, beyond my eyes.

Escapist

(পলায়নপর)

Someone wants to escape- Pedaling his cycle over and over Along
the paved pitch-road Away from dwellings-
Past the cremation grounds. Past the river
As far as one could go.

How far is it possible to go How far, for an escapist? Can he
escape the lights of the glowing skies
or the call of the clouds-their elegance,
the pitter-patter dance of incessant rains?

To speak the truth-
it is under those lights, striking sunbeams, drenched in showers
bathed in moonshine that he paves,
deeper and deeper, his escape route.

The Beggar

(কাঙাল)

Failing, falling, day after day the man who shrivels
into an earthworm -
He, who hides his sorry face from the unforgiving glare of the
days-
Once darkness falls, he's a deadly viper spewing his venom of
boundless love through fangs he's grown overnight.

His poison breeds flowers, born of rage,
of sorrow,
of a thousand distress.
You, who stand vanquished- Come strip those petals away-Tear
and rip, destroy until there's nothing left and you turn into-
A beggar of love.

A Doppelganger's Dream

(একজন ভণ্ডের স্বপ্ন)

In the swelling seas of hypocrites, I, too, perhaps, have a role.
My tongue speaks a language different from my soul.
Like two brothers bickering forever under a common roof.
Sworn to never, see the other.

When my hands come together to clap in sync with the beats of
the masses, galore-
I huddle then, in silence, in the dark room I've built inside my core.
If a narrow streak of gentle moonlight happens to invade through
the dark, the outside me then turns melancholic;
Indifferent too- not knowing where to go, losing my path-
yet, that very path, in that moment, lies within me, bathed in the
stream of gentle moonbeam.

Floating on this river of popular flow, would there come
a day of truce
when bickering brothers of the common roof
will turn around, forget disputes, face each other, and embrace?
Shake hands too?

On such a day, I shall stand alone resolute like a resilient rock
on the sandy shores of humanity.
And on that day, my tongue shall once again begin to speak the
language of my soul.

Silhouette

(সিল্যুট)

A completely failed man with no option other than
hanging himself from a ceiling fan-has just one fear –
"What if I survive?"

A completely successful man whose success is chronicled in syllabi texts-
has also just one fear-"What if I die?"

Taking these two men with him, the last man went to the fields-
dug up the earth to make a hole and gave the men
his sweat-smeared soil and told them then
"Come, bury your fears in this hole."

Saying these words, the last man left.
Carrying on his shoulders his wooden pickaxe.
Walking towards the crimson sunset He became, a silhouette.

Becoming Nero

(নিরোর মত)

The air has turned heavier with time, waiting for something to explode somewhere.

A worm, tiptoes along the tree grazing the leaves, noiselessly.

Ceaseless gurgles from a distant brook sound more and more like marching boots.

Nearing the city. Closing in.

A curfew, unannounced, looms over this earth
as I keep hunting
for a perfect hideout.

To escape, unseen, and play my violin.

Still I Fly

(তবু বিহঙ্গ)

Deep within my innermost core In spellbound awe,
I kneel before the greatness of my Inevitable Death

I sprinkle my tears-fallen petals-
over this moss-green emptiness. On the epitaph of my memories.

What else could I have done with these perishable palms, silent
sorrows?

And yet, there is life- in signs that are left And yet, there is zest In
the wings, that glide from one horizon
to the next.

Death- Unplugged

(আনপ্লাগড্ মৃত্যু)

Under the cascading brook of an unplugged death-A death, without deadlines to be met-
is drenched- every moment, every living breath.The bagpipe of Hamlin, now irrelevant.

What's left Unsaid

(না বলা কথা)

Do all those unuttered words disappear in one lifetime?
There is so much still, left unsaid.
So many words, secured in notes
left in pockets to be uttered someday.

One utters only what's measured with care. And words that lie
beyond measurement are left untouched as scribbled notes
peeping from a forgotten shirt pocket.

And then on a day of ceaseless showers every unsaid syllable
escapes the pocket to
get drenched in the rains.
To drown in the rains and turn into fragrant jasmines that freely
fall… To turn into dreams that hover upon the eye lids of a man
long gone.

All that remains unsaid-All those words-
Are never dead.

Moon Drenched

The Well

(কুয়ো)

The water remains
in the furthest depth-
The world of lights- far above. A pulleyed rope, all day long-
attends to their endless trade.

When night falls, a disarrayed moon along with her household of
stars gently surrounds the solitary well.

From the depths of darkness the water, then climbs,
to reach the riverine dying moonshine- and get drenched. Again.
Again.

Unblinking

(নিষ্পলক)

The perishability of our numbered days-
Ashen clouds of silent reproach drape the horizon, its endless
space.

What else, tell me, can I give?
Other than my cosmos of infinite sorrow?

Our existence- a mere fistful speck, fades into eternal silence...
buried in the bosom
of imperishable flames.

All that remains is a universe
of eyes that stare.
Unwept. Unblinking.

Iftaar

(ইফতার)

The moon, this night - An aluminum saucer suspended in the
skies.
Empty, quite empty without its platter. No starry grains of rice.

The starless plate pours a steady light,
which, among us, we divide
to end our Ramadan fast tonight.

Silent Feet

(নিঃশব্দ চরণে)

The mole beside your lips is a moon that sprinkles showers of
gentle light..
I let them pour
and drench my core throughout the watery night.

When dawn's early glow unfastens the window of your steadfast eyes,
I watch in them, my sunrise.

And this Is how I swim daily across the river of your body.

On the moonlit night, after everyone goes into to the wild

(জ্যোৎস্নারাতে সবাই বনে চলে গেলে)

On this moonlit night, after everyone's left for the wilderness,
I feel desolate. So lonely.
The drunken breeze of Spring sweetness turns suddenly
into a violent whirlwind having crooned and crooned tragic
melodies.

This aching heart is hurled into an endless well, and as I fall
through the abyss, I see
a solitary moon, sinking as well,
in the bottomless blue of the gleaming sky.
Sinking too, just like me-on the moonlit night when everyone's
gone into the wild.

The Rain

(বৃষ্টি)

Rain outside Rain within Tireless showers
Raindrops pouring Teardrops streaming No difference lies 'tween
them, today.

A wall- is breaking. Another -rising, Walls- all around Of rain
Of tears. Whispering Whimpering Wailing walls

A lone man- drenched to the core-as the showers pour.
Water -the surest sign of life. Drenched - to the bones.
Again, and again.
This is how one must scale the season of ruthless rain.

All Alone

(একা যে)

Let my fire stay mine alone Why must you be burning too?   This
life is a vast endless desert. But the flames have no clue.

Let my monsoon, stay mine alone
Why should the showers drench you too?
Not mere water, it's death itself with its wild, verdant hue.

Let my life be mine alone
Why must you claim a part or more? This skyless despair belongs
to my heartland, bankrupt to the core.

What that letter meant

(সে চিঠির মানে)

A letter that implies an afternoon
of solitary delights
or perhaps, an evening of fading lights.
A letter that could also mean cobblestone streets
of Irrigation Colony- A letter with the whiff of night-jasmines-
and silent anticipation or a bicycle standing quite alone.

A letter that really means-me scavenging
through my soul.

The abandoned letterbox lives on with such worthless futility-
in the shadows
of that unsent letter.
All those gigabytes
wasting away - trying to prevent the deletion of
all that was received and sent.

I stand, defeated- failing to trace
the slightest flicker of flawless flames
that could set my life ablaze.

A Speck of Gentle Sunlight

(এক চিলতে নরম রোদ)

A crow flies down to perch upon
the fence of rigid prohibition.
Carrying a speck of gentle sunshine.
Turns its head
to scavenge through
the world of prohibition.Then flies away taking the leftovers,
stinking, in the tight hollow between the beaks.
Leaving behind
at the threshold of prohibition, the tiny sunlight it once held.

A lone cat rubs herself
with the sunlit speck.
In search for
a wee-bit warmth.

After all the loving is over

(ভালোবাসাবাসি শেষ হলে)

After all the loving Is over I comehere. Here, to the riverside
like the shepherd boy who sits alone
with his feet dipped into the gentle heart-of flowing waters.
Lost in his own, doleful thoughts.

All the sadness floats away. The joy too. So does love.
There is no returning home from here, breaking the meandering
castle of dunes. All one can do, is walk away.
Walk with nothingness in the soul. Towards the river, one walks
forever. After all the loving is over.

The Vast Nothingness

(হে মহাশূন্য)

The peerless despair that hides in disguise behind the veil
of every word, proposed-I accept, touch,
feel it against
the vast emptiness of my soul.

And I find an endless cosmic space filled with nothing but
emptiness far beyond the world of words,
far beyond the propositions- suspended like an infinite sky
showing the meaning of Existence!

The Carnal World

(মাংসের দুনিয়া)

I watch blue films every night.
I lure the hungry caged animal in me with raw temptations of the
flesh.
The animal ravages itself then. Rapes over and over again.
While I sleep
like a thorough gentleman. Dawn breaks.
Morning comes.
The gentlemen on the world herd together
towards the waterbed. Gaze at their reflections in the liquid
mirror.
They don't find any animal in there.

In the carnal world-a lone hyena begins to laugh.

The Mountain Of Tears

(কান্না পাহাড়)

Every day,
I open my eyes to see the mountain of tears staring back at me.

At the top of the hill is a temple built
for the Goddess of Tears.
If the deity is pleased by the prayers,
there comes an end to human tears.

This is why I pray. My eyes run out of water, I find.
The Goddess has been kind.

And then I watch as the hill rises higher and higher, beneath my
chest.
Grows into a mountain. Hard and steep.

I have lost the power to weep.

The Journey

Playtime

(খেলা যখন)

Abandonment drags me now to faraway lands with endless shores
of saline sands
carrying songs of the ocean within.

How much longer must I be dragged? How much poorer must I
get?
The fire in my blood, is still ablaze.No end to this burning yet.

O my Abandonment, leave me be. Let go of my tethered identity.
O my Desire,
Face me now. Let me thrive in fleeting moments that hold the
wonderous pleasures
of the game called Life.

Before the Departure

(যাবার আগে)

Before I departI take with me
the dull glow of fading twilight that lingers on your soft forehead.

I leave behind
our cumulative savings
moments stifled with unwept tears splintered shards of broken
dreams perpetual patterns-
restless, yet stagnant. I leave these behind just for you.

After all, this is no way to depart. Is any departure possible, at all?
I know.. I know..
Still I leave.. Still I go...

Taking with me nothing beyond a lingering touch
of that dull afterglow.

Postman

(পোস্টম্যান)

In this digital age, a postman waits
In the forests of Autumn-Waits in eternal exile.
He's now a wordless tree.

His silent heart, is swollen with leaves Yellowing leaves that wilt
and wither In the ruthless autumn breeze.

Leaves that will drown someday into the warmth
of the embracing earth
To be nourished and loved into another sapling
on a different Spring.

O Virgin Life

(হে অনূঢ় জীবন)

In every shadow you leave as you tread your path,
I find a darkness to hide my face.

Every time you cross the realms of my sight I stand grazing
the boundary lines.

And when you
slow down to reach your senile state,
I am silenced too, then, by your deathliness.

My Virgin Life!

Anticlimax

(অ্যান্টিক্লাইমেক্স)

The caller tune repeats a song of dying words

Every sound carries
an anticlimax of silence.

Every relationship carries an etherized damage.
Countless words flutter their wings
and float in urgent futility in a muted sky
that has no reply.

Relationships decorate the living room
the flower-vase and bed

The damage, shoved deftly under the carpet.

Railway Tracks

(রেললাইন)

Two tracks lying in parallel.
Pristine emptiness filling their gaps. Who knows where they begin.
Or end.

It's only the air that grows heavier.
Laden with
the weeping sighs
of approaching whistles from faraway lands.

Surrender...

(সারেন্ডার...)

After abandoning your worldly wealth
After watching them float away, you turned around. And found
nothing but
a penniless road ahead.

The road bought off all your smartness.
All your badass attitude.
All it gave you in return
was the right to turn destitute.

You really have no option left save treading this path
that has no destination.

Watch now your waving hands Watch how they willingly flaunt
the pristine banner of submission!

The Wick

(সলতে)

The glowing wick of life is a friend of night.
Days are devoid of love.

The day is like gleaming sunlight. Transparent and real. No magic
there. Night knows how to cast her spell.
The world of the surreal.

The day spins the wheels of life into an endless race.
Night is when love blooms again in silent grace.

All that was true during the night- turns into farce in dazzling
daylight. And in this space,
between the nights and days-
the wick of life oscillates.

The Storm

(ঝড়)

I am walking through a storm. An enormous storm.
Violent gusts, hurled at me. Endlessly.

The absence of a storm is also a storm;
a storm that hides, brews inside.
Prowls in silence, waiting to pounce. I run. I flee.
I fall. I rise.
I run again. Again and again. The storm doesn't let me be.

One day, I halt. I cease to run. The storm too takes a pause,
and comes to rest by my side
like a pet cat, purring slow.

I gently stroke its furry head. It falls asleep.
So do I.

Immersion

(বিসর্জন)

I indulge in a few chosen wounds. Every day, I say-
Come- Dig deeper into my hurting and celebrate your gluttonous
appetite. Come, rip me apart from inside out.
Leave, however, a fleeting ray of consciousness
nestled in the branches-a tiny morsel of leftover from your festive
feast.

Come- scorch me more, with your flames. Cremate me here- by
the riverside.
Let me, my ashes, my consciousness be immersed in this ocean
of eternal joy.

The Dope of Infinity

(অনন্তের নেশা)

I see nothing Yet I see
Not seeing is also a vision of sorts.

I say nothing Yet I say
Not saying is also
a language of sorts.

I am rooted here- between these worlds of speech and silence,
vision and blindness.

And yet,
the dope of infinity keeps me high.
Makes me flutter endlessly-
from the flagpole of my existence.

Birdsong

(পাখির গান)

A candle burns- melts away Soon its fire will be out.
And then
In the lightless dark, a pair of eyes
shall begin to glow.
The body will emerge from behind the shadow.
The face
behind the mask, as well.

And we shall march from one darkness into another.

When will dawn finally break? Hand in hand. Shoulders, nesting
the tired head.
That kind of dawn? When? When will the birds, sing again?

The Poet

Shredded Verse

(ছেঁড়া কবিতা)

Although the poem was ripped apart-The wailing heart could not
be torn.

One is surrounded by dark-hands one cannot reach; at times
though a tiny speck of fragmented light
slips in through the knuckled window-to draw patterns that
become poetry.

The wailing heart like a tamed convict
waits behind the iron bars.

The wailing heart is a marked criminal
Don't let it ever escape. Don't ever set it free.

It's better you tear the poem instead.

Feline

(বেড়াল)

No matter how much fire is spewed
By the wild and fiery Flame Of The Forest No poetry, Boss, is
happening, this Spring.

A famished cat
is carefully crossing hurdles of
splintered glass that trail along the fence;
she measures the wind with her feline tail.

Down on the streets,
bloodhounds of the neighborhood, howl baring their teeth, they
scream and scowl to rip open the hungry feline's
jugular vein. To play Holi,
with the rawness of her sprinkled blood.

Is poetry even a thing, tell me,
in such a perilous Spring?

Yet, in this very Spring, every shard of broken glass from the
fences of the world
turns into fish under the paws of every famished, craving cat. And
this, to me, is Poetry!

The days of the Cumulonimbus

(কুমুলোনিম্বাসের দিন)

As I write, my unwept tears yearn to turn into poetry.
Shattered shards, from deep inside strive to scale the stairs of
words and reach the pinnacle
of consciousness.

When the season of
the cumulonimbus arrives
to fill my blank pages, again- words wipe away more words.
And, in the pitter-patter of gentle erasure-
I discover-
a poem arising from the mist A poem- out of the fogginess.
It comes, it comes it comes to me-
in the shape of infinite emptiness.

Joke of a Poem

(কবিতার ইয়ার্কি)

You are the Nation And I, Sedition!

There is peace in your giving And violence in my Singing!

You fire the shells, bullets. I just have rocks, you see-
teardrops hardened through decades of treachery!

You have in your hands- the iron rod And I, my hunger to survive.
Can hunger be governed, can it be tamed? Is bread, only yours to
be claimed!

You define Harmony And I, Anarchy!
If you are Democracy Then I, the muted History!

Our battles are unequal. On different planes. This poem, alas, a
mockery.

An Author, Really !

(সত্যি লেখক)

People read books- fictions and tales- I, for one, read only humans
Page after page- I turn them over like a ravenous bookworm, I
devour humans of different dimensions.
So many around me, of different binds I hoard them every second
in my mind.

I read through the day, through endless nights The beggar man at
the traffic lights
The vendor with the weighing-scale at the market, the garbage
collector, the lovesick, heartbroken survivor the angry one, the
amicable, as well- My palate is home to every kind.

I read. I read.
And some day
I end up reading myself too, to determine, finally-
If I there is indeed a poet in me.

Statue of Light

(আলোর প্রতিমা)

Shall I only utter words of melancholy?

What about the cosmic stars in the gardens of the universe?

What about the petals they gently sprinkle into the despondent dark?

And the poet who bathes in the pollens of light to fall in love with every day,

Shall I never write of his daily delight?

This is why

I chisel through

the heart of rock-hard despondence to carve a statue of luminance.

My country

(আমার দেশ)

This land that lies
under the weight of power is not my country.

My country
Is the sky that is caressed by the glow of dawn
Is the earth that is covered by the moonlit night
Is the meandering flow of every river
Is the symphony
of the cascading streams.

My country
Is the labor of men on barren land Is the scent of crops filling the
fields
Is the humming of birds to which they rise-The hills and oceans,
the countryside.

My country lives
in a morsel of fistful rice
held at the mouths of starving men .

My country is not
its concocted democracy.
My country is not
its churches, temples or mosques. My country is free-
as free as the liberal sky.

My country is
Your unpartitioned heart.

An impossible Poem

(একটি অসম্ভব কবিতা)

The eyes yearn
for an impossible poem.

Sometimes,
when a syllable or two, trickle down their corners and fall
unawares,
don't dismiss them for ordinary tears.

Instead, let your expression be that of inevitable awe
for this chimera of dancing lights.

Let the unwritten syllables
find their way
to infinity
let them sail away
on the wings of melancholic breeze.

Perhaps at dusk
when the daylights dim you shall find their glow in the elusive
cosmos
of constellations, again.

Perhaps in the stillness of a solitary evening…

The Starry Night

(দ্য স্টারি নাইট)

I borrowed a few words of vibrant hue
from Van Gogh's palette to paint a whirlwind poem on the canvas
of your skin.

All night long, constellations of yellow, surrendered
to the easel of flesh. And, the deep cobalt sky grew beyond your
body to paint a night
of brilliant stars.

Let me say just this

(একটা ছোট কথা ছিল)

Let me say just this- I have no pain in me.
I just keep rubbing
the greasy darkness of the sky into my palms, all my life.

Let me say just this -
I have no sorrow in me.
I just keep getting
bone-drenched as I walk through this endless fog losing my way,
all my life.

Let me say just this -
I have no joy as well, in me.
I just keep rubbing
the orange of the sinking sun into my palms before it drowns in
the bosom of the dusky river.

I have nothing else to say.

Indestructible

(ন হন্যতে)

A darkness prepares. Readies itself. Just for me, my waiting self.

How long can a traveler walk down the tumultuous line of life braving endless ups and downs to lose every fleeting waterborne dream?

Is there still a thing called death? After all that's gone and lost? One doesn't know. One can't. Therefore, giving the dimensions of death a miss, one prepares for a different darkness.
A darkness that runs on parallel tracks. A darkness that has built itself-

Just for me, my waiting self.

There is More

(আরো কিছু)

There is more than meets the eye Secret, furtive robberies, too-
Sun and Shade play peek-a-boo.

There is more than meets the eye Hidden pangs of this heartland
Tales of water beneath the sand.

There is no more debt, no loan-
At day-end all that beckons is
the endless sky waving me home.

And then, all that is left to traverse, transcends the known limits
of death This earth, brick-red alleys of dust strewn with life- its
indelible lust.

Milton Keynes UK
Ingram Content Group UK Ltd.
UKHW040825250224
438359UK00004B/155

9 789359 894492